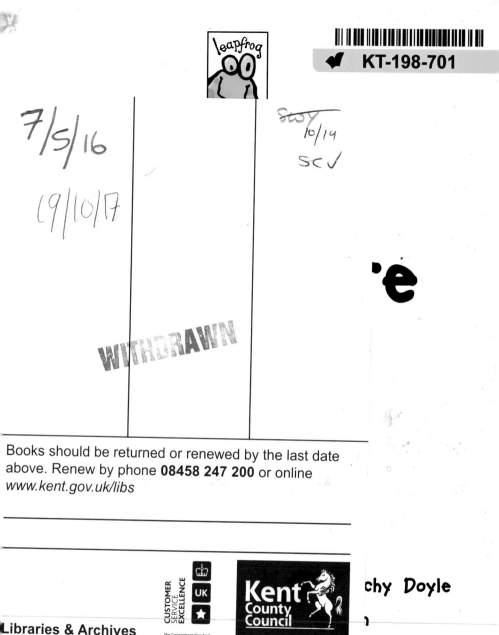

leapfrog

7/5/16

(9/10/17

10/14

SC ✓

'e

WITHDRAWN

Books should be returned or renewed by the last date
above. Renew by phone **08458 247 200** or online
www.kent.gov.uk/libs

CUSTOMER
SERVICE
EXCELLENCE
The Government Standard

Kent
County
Council

01128\DTP\RN\11.10   LIB 7

...chy Doyle

Libraries & Archives

W
FRANKLIN WATTS

First published in 2010 by
Franklin Watts
338 Euston Road
London
NW1 3BH

Franklin Watts Australia
Level 17/207 Kent Street
Sydney
NSW 2000

A CIP catalogue record for this book is available
from the British Library.

ISBN 978 0 7496 9415 9 (hbk)
ISBN 978 0 7496 9421 0 (pbk)

Series Editor: Jackie Hamley
Editor: Melanie Palmer
Series Advisor: Catherine Glavina
Series Designer: Peter Scoulding

Printed in China

To find out more about Malachy
Doyle and his books, please visit:
www.malachydoyle.com

Franklin Watts is a division of
Hachette Children's Books,
an Hachette UK company.
www.hachette.co.uk

This tale comes from North America. Can you find this on a map?

A long time ago,
Bluebird wasn't blue.
She was plain white.

One day, she came to a
lake. "I wish I was blue,
like you!" cried the bird.

So she jumped into the water, singing:

"Here is still water,
clear and blue.
In I go, now I'm blue too!"

She did the
same thing
for three days.

8

9

On the third day, she came out of the water with blue feathers!

Coyote had been
watching.
"I want to be blue,
too," he said.

So he jumped into
the lake, singing
Bluebird's song:

"Here is still water,
clear and blue.
In I go, now I'm blue too!"

Coyote did the
same thing for
three days.

18

On the third day, he
looked at himself in
the water ...

"I'm blue! I'm blue!" cried Coyote. And he ran to show Bluebird.

But he was so busy
admiring himself that
he didn't watch where
he was going.

He bumped into a tree
and bounced straight back
onto the muddy road.

Then a great wind blew
and Coyote was covered
in mud and dust.
"Oh no!" he cried. His fur
was dirty and brown.

Coyotes have been
the colour of
the dusty earth
ever since.

Puzzle 1

Put these pictures in the correct order.
Now tell the story in your own words.
What different endings can you think of?

Puzzle 2

happy   shy
proud

foolish   careful
hasty

Choose the correct words for each character. Which words are incorrect? Turn over to find the answers.

Answers

Puzzle 1

The correct order is 1c, 2e, 3f, 4a, 5d, 6b

Puzzle 2

Bluebird: the correct words are happy, proud

The incorrect word is shy

Coyote: the correct words are foolish, hasty

The incorrect word is careful

Look out for Leapfrog World Tales:

*hardback